IF I HAD A VOICE LIKE …
AND OTHER SHORT STORIES

by

JERRY DEAN PATE

DEDICATION

For: Anne, Bryan, Deborah, Dusty, Kevin, Maggie, Rick & Van

CHAPTER 1

IF I HAD A VOICE LIKE …

J.C. Loomis was the afternoon drive man at WRAT radio in Ratbait, SC, and the hottest thing around. He was doing a remote and interviewing one of the sales ladies at the local department store. The door burst open, and a horde of teenage girls came pouring through. They shoved women aside and interrupted the conversation.

"J.C., sign my book."

"Somebody take my picture."

"J.C., you're so cute," one of them said, as the girls pressed him against a counter filled with women's panties and girdles.

"Um, look girls," he said, "listen to Mrs. Carpenter tell you about these latest items they have on sale."

"No, we wanna talk to you."

He was trying to figure out how to regain control, held up a girdle and asked, "You girls wear these?"

"Yes!" they chorused.

"Tell me why?" he asked, and a summary of benefits turned the interruption into a commercial.

"It makes me slimmer."

"I feel dressed up."

"I can wear stockings."

"My momma said I had to."

"Thank you, girls. Folks, come on down to Belk's. We'll switch back to the station now. We got some music for you."

"Yay!" said the girls, and the music started.

J.C. signed autographs, got hugged, and thanked the girls for listening to his show. He was WRAT's biggest star. In just three short months, he'd increased his audience and sales to record numbers. On top of his popularity, he'd been damned from the pulpit by the preacher at Westside Baptist Church. "He's lewd-uh, crewed-uh, and intent on wrecking the moral fiber of this community."

J.C. Loomis was a hit!

Growing up in a dirt-floored shack, he quit tenth grade to get away from his drunk father. He joined the Army. When he got out, he bought a pair of cowboy boots, grew sideburns like Elvis, and bought a customized Mercury convertible. It had dual exhausts and mufflers that would suck back when he revved the engine.

When he left Ft. Bragg, he drove straight to Charlotte and enrolled in the Carolina School of Broadcasting. Five weeks and $457 later, he had a certificate saying he was qualified to work at any radio station in the country.

J.C. could ad lib with the best of them and had the fastest hands of any DJ around. He could cue up two records and three tapes, find the next live commercial in the copy book, and dump the ash tray, all while reading the weather forecast.

Weather forecasts were easy, but when it came to reading anything else, J.C. had problems. His personality would shift, his voice would get deeper, and he would become careful to say his words just so. He preferred to work from a factsheet rather than read copy, and he hated reading newscasts.

His dream was to get to Nashville and WSM. He loved Ralph Emery.

"He's one of the finest people you'd ever want to meet," he told a lady friend. "I introduced him once at the Pickens Country Music Festival. Bill Anderson was headlining along with Loretta Lynn. Loretta was so pregnant with her twins, she had to pick her guitar way up on her belly. The crowd loved her."

"That night Emery told me, 'Kid, you have to be ready when your break comes. You need to be working every kind of show you can. Whether it's something like tonight, a talent show, a beauty contest, or anything else, you'll get more and more experience before a live audience. Once you've put in the time, then the talent, and I think you have the talent, will come through.'"

After that, J.C. worked everywhere he could. On Tuesday nights, he did a record hop at the Atomic Circus Skating Rink. On Thursdays, it was the 6:20 Club with Red Reynolds and his Rainbow Valley Boys. Friday night, he taped his play-by-play of the Ratbait Red Raiders football game. Even on dates, he'd park at the Circle C restaurant, listen to Ralph Emery, and introduce records along with him.

"Listen to that," he told his lady friend. "I wish I had a voice like that. If I had a voice like that, I could be in Nashville making money off P.I. spots like the big boys do."

"P.I. spots?"

"You make money per inquiry, like Randy's Record Shop commercials. That guy gets a percentage of every record that's ordered. Yes, sir, if I had a voice like that, I'd be living in one of them big houses next to Dolly Parton."

"I think your voice is fine," she cooed.

"Naw, for the big time, you need a deep voice like Ralph Emery or T. Tommy. If I had a voice like T. Tommy, I could work the big time."

"I read in a movie magazine that Lauren Bacall hung across an exercise bar and yelled to lower hers. You could try that if you must, but I think your voice is just fine."

The next day, J.C. laid over a sawhorse in the garage and yelled into a burlap bag. It just made him hoarse. When he noticed that smokers had deeper voices, he bought a pack of Camels, smoked, and smoked until he got addicted—no change.

In the Circle C. parking lot, there were more intros, along with Ralph Emery. His date hugged him close and whispered, "I told you, you've got a nice voice already; there's no need to change it. Maybe what you need is some gimmick, something different from everybody else."

That was it. He found it on a back wall in the pawn shop. It was one of those old-timey car horns with a rubber bulb on the end. It was perfect. It sounded like a goose.

Armed with this new tool, he showed up at the skating rink. The taped intro included sound effects as the announcer said, "Welcome to the Atomic Circus Skating Rink—*KER-BLOOM-YOW!!*—and now here's the sensational, Jay-ceeee Loooooomissssss."

HONK-HONK-HONK!!—J.C. squeezed the BLAP horn and shouted, "Hi guys and gals, this is old J.C., your man with the plan for you to have fun tonight. Here's the first skate of the evening, ladies' choice: Roy Orbison sings 'Make Believe'."

Some young boys began racing through the crowd. J.C. hollered, "Hey—*HONK-HONK!!*—you kids, slow down, skate in the middle, and skate to your left."

The Evans Mill boys were on the floor. J.C. didn't like them. They could skate well, and he couldn't. More importantly, they were skating with girls who would never speak to them at school but readily accepted their invitation here.

Homer Beagley was one of the mill boys on the floor. J.C. didn't like him. Homer could skate forward with a slow, stretching crossover step that the girls liked, and he could skate backwards and hold a girl like a dancer. He won all the races held between the first and second skates each Tuesday. But J.C. noticed that Homer often made younger kids spin out on the turns.

Tall and skinny, Homer had bad teeth. His clothes were sometimes dirty, but his Chico Revera Championship shoe skates were always spit-shined to a patent leather finish. They were highlighted with military-police-styled white leather laces.

Homer was a quiet boy; he did not like loud people, especially J.C. Loomis. J.C. honked the horn, and Homer erupted, "You blow that horn at me one more time, and I'm gonna stick it up your ass!"

The little kids knew there was bad blood between the two. "I told J.C.," one of them said, "that Homer forced me outside during the race last week. He said the next time it happened, he was going to throw Homer off the floor. You wait, J.C. is gonna stop Homer from cheating."

A group of Baptist kids from Spartanburg had come over, which, when combined with the regulars, packed the rink with skaters. Fat Toby Robertson, owner of the Atomic Circus, told J.C. to really lean on traffic control. "Keep 'em moving. Work the beginners to the middle, and don't let them start that crack-the-whip shit."

J.C. circled the crowd to the left with "Loving You" and upped the tempo a little with the Platters' "Magic Touch", and, when the crowd settled in, he jumped them to Chuck Berry and "Rock and Roll Music". The guitar cut through the grind of wheels on the floor, and skaters bounded. Some tried to match the—*CHUNKA-CHUNKA-CHUNKA!!*—rhythm of the bass pounding across the hoods of cars and echoing clear out to the tree line a half mile away.

The crowd was under his control and his command. It was like he could get people to buy White Rose Petroleum Jelly, Cardui tablets, and Sister Esther's Love Tonic. It was the J.C. Loomis show, live from WSM, home of the Grand Ole Opry!

He honked at a snooty girl, who gave him a dirty look. She rolled by again and got another honk. On the next record, J.C. dedicated it to her. "This one goes out to Martha Snell from Jonesville; here's Pat Boone and 'Love Letters in the Sand'."

Homer Beagley cut through the center poles and caught her. Clasping hands, they glided stride for stride like Loons in a mating rite. They passed the booth; J.C. honked the horn and grinned.

When the first skate ended, Fat Toby dust-mopped the rink's floor. The younger boys knew that was the prelude to the race and gathered at the corner of the third turn to check it out. It looked fast and slick. They waited for J.C. to announce the start.

"Alright, ladies and gentlemen, this is the boy's race for tonight. The winner gets three skates for free anytime this week. The rules are no crack the whip, no cutting through the center, and," J.C. looked at Homer, "no shoving."—*HONK-HONK-HONK!!*

"Alright, five laps around. Now move up to the center, where Toby will start you." The boys clattered along an imaginary line from Toby's shoe to the side of the tent.

Those new to skating in a rink stood sideways to the line. The older, more experienced skaters perched like ballet dancers on their toe-breaks for a running start. "One, two, three, go!"

Three boys fell at the line, while a red-haired eight-year-old flailed his arms as he took oversized steps to get moving. The Lowery twins were pushing and shoving each other as the line of skaters moved forward like a big freighter pulling out of Spartanburg Yard.

Flying ahead of the group was a stiletto-thin figure with black boots and white laces. His head low, he pulled his arms in perfect coordination with strides pressing to build speed.

Homer Beagley eased into a cross-legged stride through the first corner. He made the turn just as he planned, legs and hips at an angle, shoulders parallel to the floor. Down the straightaway, he sped.

He eased off in the fourth turn and felt confident he could pass the field at least once before the final lap. Suddenly, something flickered on his left.

He'd learned never to look back. Someone could fake a move on one side and pass on the other. He took the turn wide for a better view. It wasn't there. Then it was—and on his left side too. Down the straightaway, he pushed, pushed too hard, and broke stride. In the second turn, with less than three laps to go, he saw the flicker again. This time it was more frequent, rhythmical, pulsating, and pumping. It grew bigger and bigger. Homer bore down. It flickered again. It was a finger, another pump, a hand, a pump, an arm, then a shoulder.

The red-haired eight-year-old was inches away when Homer looked behind himself. The kid dropped into a crouch, skating, skating, skating. He matched Homer, stride for stride. As they crabbed into the fourth turn, the kid did a short skip, forcing Homer to break stride. The eight-year-old broke free. J.C. hollered, "Keep going Red; you got him!"—*HONK-HONK-HONK!!*

The youngster started a cross-over crab when a Cobra-like shadow loomed over him. As they shot towards the corner, the youngster hit the rail and flipped over onto the dirt parking lot. *HONK-HONK-HONK!!*—The horn sounded. "Disqualified," J.C. yelled, "for unsportsmanlike conduct."

"You son of a bitch! I told you not to blow that horn at me!" Homer yelled.

He took a swing, but J.C. ducked and then whanged the BLAP horn off Homer's head like a pipe hitting a steel pole. Homer fell backwards. A woman screamed, and a boy yelled, "Homer needs help!" Two of them jumped J.C. from the back of the booth.

The microphone was knocked to the floor, and noise of the fight played over the PA system. A man from Spartanburg dove in and pulled one boy off. J.C. hit the other before Homer rolled up. Records sprayed to the floor, and a recording of "Hound Dog" blared over the loudspeakers.

J.C. jumped out of the booth and knocked Homer flat. Mill boys poured over the rails. Girls were crying; mothers were yelling, "Get in this car; they gonna kill somebody! Call the sheriff!"

Fat Toby tried to get them back over the rail and got knocked down.

J.C. had Homer's mouth bleeding, then saw the flash of a switchblade in another boy's hand.

A truck driver from Pageland saw it too and cut the tent's main rope. A cloud of canvas shushed down over J.C., Homer, and the boy with the knife.

It was quiet. Headlights turned on. A spotlight from a pickup searched beneath the rails. The skating rink looked like a dehydrated elephant. Nothing moved for a minute or so. Slowly, men and boys began crawling out. In the distance, a siren slipped through the night air.

J.C. lost his job at the Atomic Circus. The Reabuck Ministerial Association threatened to launch a boycott against the radio station if the owner did not fire him. The sheriff ran Toby Roberts off. Rumors came out sometime later that Fat Toby got killed in Georgia by some woman's husband.

J.C. spent three months looking for a job. The wire services carried the story of the fight all over the state, and no radio station would hire him. He got on as a car hop at the Circle C drive-in, where he spends his evenings waiting on cars and doing intros with Ralph Emery. To this day, he tells anyone who'll listen, "Hear that? If I had a voice like that, I could make a fortune."

CHAPTER 2

THE GREAT WHITE WHALE

When Battery D assembled, a family stood at one end of the armory. There was a father, a mother, and six girls standing in a line by age and height. They were watching Clebert Caldwell snap to attention and listening as the First Sergeant began calling a role.

When Clebert yelled, "Here," they clapped.

The First Sergeant barked, "Fall out and get on the trucks." Clebert hoisted his duffle bag, kissed his mother, said "Bye" to his father and sisters, then went outside to load up. Battery D, a national guard unit, was about to convoy from Anderson, SC, to the Army's largest military post down below Savannah, Georgia.

As the trucks rolled out the gate, Clebert's family stood waving, "Bye Clebert," as Clebert grinned and waved. At the city limits, his family was waving and hollering, "Bye Clebert." As the convoy rode out from Augusta, Georgia, they were there again. At Waynesboro, they "Bye Clebert-ed," then Millen, "Bye Clebert," Statesboro, "Bye Clebert," and Pembroke. Finally, they waved "Bye Clebert" as the convoy drove into the main gate of Fort Stewart.

Clebert Caldwell had been in the National Guard eight years. With great effort, he had risen to the rank of Specialist Fourth Class. The Guard did not trust Clebert to lead troops, fire guns, or light cookstoves. He was used for lifting. Whereas it took four men to set the autoloaders outside the turret of a 40mm antiaircraft gun, Clebert could do it by himself in one grunt.

He became famous for his trademark "What kind of deal is this?" one night when a drunk soldier staggered into the wrong barracks and tried to get into a bunk with Clebert in it. Clebert slung the drunk who landed with a giant—*SPLAT!!* Clebert jumped out of bed and shouted, "What kind of deal is this?" as he pulled his drawers up. Someone turned on the lights, and the frightened soldier ran out the door.

Clebert was massive. He had red, curly hair and broad shoulders atop a big, hairy chest and belly. Despite his bulk, he had a high, squeaky voice. Except for the First Sergeant and the unit clerk, none of the troops knew his first name or that his momma had named him in honor of her brothers, Cleveland and Herbert. The troops called him Whale, or when formality required, The Great White Whale.

Clebert was in an antiaircraft artillery battery of M42 Dusters, lightly armored tanks with two 40mm Bofors guns mounted on top. The guns blew away lots of Jap zeroes during WWII but were now obsolete because the barrels couldn't swing fast enough to hit jet planes.

Despite this, a congressman insisted the Army let contracts go to buy Dusters by the hundreds. He had a tank chassis plant in his district and wanted to keep it going. The Army was forced to buy them but did not need them, so it dumped them on the National Guard.

There were over a hundred M42s at Fort Stewart, Georgia, a sprawling, post-WWII backwater of swamps and bogs filled with wild animals and things that bit or stunk. Besides having oppressive humidity, it rained there every afternoon around four-thirty.

Duster units fired at radio-controlled drones on artillery ranges many miles from post headquarters and human beings. It was so far out that troops bivouacked in woods near their range. The mosquitoes out there were huge. You could hear them haul a soldier out of his tent late at night and then argue whether he was big enough to eat. The place was infested with things that crept or crawled, bit, and stung. There were also deer, feral hogs, gators, and snakes. By eight-thirty p.m., the woods were dark.

There was a lot of yelling when trucks carrying Whale's unit pulled into the bivouac area that summer. Sergeants hollered, "Get out, form up by platoons." Once assembled, the First Sergeant commanded, "At ease," so the troops could swat and smack the gnats, mosquitoes, and horse flies that showed up as if they had been given the hour of a feast. The First Sergeant passed layouts of camping areas to each platoon sergeant. "Spread your men over each of these," he ordered. Then he turned and yelled, "Nick, send over Whale and that new Jervis boy."

"Get that rake, pickax, and that shovel, and come with me," he told them, then led them a short distance and stopped just behind a cluster of holly bushes. After they raked away pine straw and leaves, Whale and Jervis stomped and swatted at mosquitoes and watched the sergeant take a dead tree limb and draw two long lines in the dirt about a foot apart. "You two are gonna dig the slit trench," he said.

They picked, dug, and swatted until both of them were blowing hard. An hour later, they were done and had put the equipment away. Their shirts were stinking from sweat, and their faces were hardly recognizable with dirt smeared over big lumps of bug bites. It took a while for them to get their duffle bags and find their platoon because Blinky kept telling Whale to slow down and look for snakes.

Blinky Jervis was new to the unit. He was assigned as Whale's tent mate because he and Whale had things in common: incredible strength, mental limitations, and loud snoring. Their platoon sergeant made them set up their tent far away because of it. Private Harry T. Jervis was called Blinky due to a bad facial tic that set in when he got nervous. The blinking and twitching started when he was first in school.

The boys in the lunchroom hustled ahead of him to keep him from sitting at their table. Each time Harry tried, a boy said, "This seat is taken," or a boy behind him said, "That's my seat," and on and on until Harry was forced to sit with the girls. Even there, the gangly third grader was laughed at and teased. He was wearing hand-me-down coveralls two sizes too big. One of the girls chided, "Can you spin around inside those pants?"

When he stood to leave, a boy blocked his path, and another boy slipped a green snake inside his coveralls. This surprised Harry T. and the whole lunchroom. He tossed his tray, dropped his coveralls and his undershorts, and in front of the girls, teachers, and God, he wildly twisted, slapped, and yelled, "Snake! Snake! Snake!" to get the green serpent off his butt."

The boys howled and banged on their table. The instigator retrieved the snake and held it up, noting it was harmless. The girls were laughing and hiding their eyes when one of them observed, "Harry T. Jervis is definitely not Jewish."

Ever since then, Harry T. Jervis was terrified of snakes. He was initially dubbed Nervous Jervis by his schoolmates, but that moniker gave way to Blinky when he came down with this exaggerated nervous eye tic.

Now he was out in the woods, where he and the Great White Whale Caldwell had to sleep on the ground where bugs crawled and reptiles slithered.

Actually, no one in this unit actually slept in the dirt. They set up pup tents with the sides raised well off the ground. This was necessary to accommodate military gear and, more importantly, non-military things like lawn chairs, portable cots, beer, and beer coolers. It did not matter that they looked more like Bedouins than a military unit; these men were citizen soldiers, not regular Army.

After picking a spot, Whale and Blinky buttoned together their two-man shelter halves, then raised the sides in an elaborate arrangement of sticks, tie-offs, and pegs. Blinky slid a rusty beach chair inside, folded it back, and climbed in to try it out. It was too short.

"What kind of deal? … Can you sleep in that?" Whale asked.

"Hell, if I'm gonna get off the ground, I ain't got no choice. Set your cot in here, Whale. We may need to raise the sides some more."

Whale was too big for a lawn chair. He spread his hairy blob over a portable cot with his feet sticking out. It had wooden legs and canvas stretched over the frame, and it was almost two feet off the ground.

The two of them spent their days on the artillery range hauling ammo and lifting stuff. It was hard work and terribly hot. When the firing was done for the day, they picked up empty shells and helped crews disassemble the guns for cleaning. After this, the whole unit loaded into trucks and rode back to the bivouac area for final formation and chow.

After they finished one afternoon, Blinky and Whale retrieved their mess kits and caught the tail end of the chow line. There was animated movement ahead of them where the line bent around a two-and-a-half-ton truck. Soldiers were stopping to see a very large diamondback rattlesnake, killed earlier, that someone had stretched across the truck's bumper. At the serving area, the cooks had laid a big copperhead on tinfoil that they had killed just before chow.

Men sat around the mess truck, digging into their food, and talking … about snakes. The know-it-alls said cottonmouth moccasins hid in trees just waiting to drop into passing boats, and that angry coachwhips stuck their tails in their mouths to roll after someone. One guy bragged that he knew that snakes could reason and think and that the poisonous snakes were always trying to get even because of what happened in the Garden of Eden.

Someone pointed towards a pond in the distance and said, "A few years back, we were out here, and I saw a big-assed water moccasin crawl out that pond and chase a wild hog off the bank. Them cottonmouths are mean."

"Hell," said another, "a few years ago a copperhead bit a guy squatting over a slit trench."

By now, some had finished eating and went to the truck where the rattlesnake was laid out. They took turns, Good Ole Boy Style, holding the deceased by the tail and saying, "Take my pichur. My old lady ain't gonna believe this." One of them walked back to the mess truck and bragged he'd held the snake. "Damn thing is so big; he could knock the tires off a jeep."

Snakes dominated conversations that afternoon. Blinky Jervis crawled into the back of the mess truck, well off the ground. His eye was twitching furiously as he appealed to the heavens for protection from snakes. Just in case the prayers did not work, he planned to get enough beer in him to calm his jumpy nerves.

The cooks noticed his eye and began joking, "Damn, he's sending Morse Code."

After the mess crew cleaned up, a platoon sergeant passed out several hymn books, and a group gathered around the back of the truck to sing gospel songs and drink beer. Whale Caldwell didn't drink, but he sang tenor and was good at it. As more beer was consumed, the singing got louder, and songs were requested. "Damn, y'all sounded good on that one," someone said. "How 'bout the Old Rugged Cross?"

As the darkness came on, a Coleman lantern was lit. The group sang more hymns while popping open fresh cans of beer. When it got too dark to read the hymnals, the group decided to end their concert with Amazing Grace. Everybody sang, including the cooks and the Mess Sergeant, who motioned for Blinky to get down from the truck. He was singing along with the others as he climbed in, then got down holding a box of salt and singing, "... was blind, but now I see."

He handed Whale the salt. The cooks giggled.

"What's this for?" Whale asked.

"It's snake repellant. You and Blinky may need it if the mate of that rattlesnake comes around."

"Just pour that salt around your tent and inside where you sleep. That'll do the job."

"Better yet, pee around it. Snakes don't like the smell of pee. No snake will come near, even the mate of that rattlesnake killed earlier."

Then, as the cooks snickered, he reminded them, "You know, when their mates get killed, rattlesnakes always look for somebody they can get revenge from. Take that salt and put it out. I'm gonna pour some around the mess truck and pee around it before I turn in."

Whale passed Blinky the salt and muttered, "I ain't worried 'bout no snakes. Let's go." Blinky quivered, "Lemme get a six pack, and I'll walk out with you."

Both of them were shining flashlights, with Whale grumbling, "Hurry up," as Blinky slowly walked behind, stomping loudly, checking for things that crawled.

After looking in and around their tent, Whale stripped off his boots, pants, and shirt. He stowed them in his duffle bag and blobbed onto his cot.

Blinky pulled his beach chair out of the tent and popped open another beer.

"What kinda … you gonna drink all them beers?" Whale muttered.

"Not all of them, just a few more while I check out things."

"There ain't no snakes out here, Blinky. If there wuz, we scared them off with our stompin'. Now don't do no more stompin' Blinky; I need to get to sleep. They gonna let me load one of the guns tomorrow, and I need to rest up for it."

When Whale began snoring, Blinky shined his light and walked out some distance. He began an elaborate circling-back-to-the-tent ritual. He was shining and looking … and checking around stumps and under logs for snakes.

When he was done, he slid his lounge chair inside the tent and poured salt outside the raised sides. Then, as instructed, he relieved himself by spraying a line outside the salt. He tried to pee inside the tent but stopped when Whale chirped, "What kind of dea …?" turned over and resumed snoring.

Satisfied he had protection from that avenging snake, Blinky took off his boots, put his socks in them, and stowed them just behind his chair. He slipped off his pants, rolled his shirt into a pillow, laid back, and pulled up a damp bed sheet. In a short time, the beer in his belly had him snoring along with Whale in a chorus of grunts and snorts that could attract horny sows.

Whale was in deep sleep, dreaming about his chance of becoming a cannoneer. If he did well with that, he dreamt he would be assigned to a gun crew, which meant he'd no longer be hauling ammo. After all, he was a Spec Four.

By now, Blinky was in REM sleep, with realistic dreams rising in his brain. In it, a light rain was falling, keeping away mosquitoes, flies, and ants ... and washing off his snake repellant.

He dreamt he was outside his own body and could see this giant rattlesnake slowly easing into the tent towards him. Blinky was hollering at himself, but nothing came out ... nothing. He watched the rattler slither up the chair and saw the snake smile, then struck at his face. Now Blinky had a voice.

"Snake, Snake!" he yelled. "I been bit by a snake!" and stood up—*stood up*—inside a two-man pup tent. Pegs and cords pulled loose, and canvas draped over his head and his whole body. As he thrashed and twisted, a tent peg struck his mouth. "Oh, Jesus, he bit me again!" Blinky yelled, convinced he could not see because a giant Fort Stewart rattlesnake was wrapped around his head, trying to bite him dead.

Whale shouted, "What kind of deal is this?" and leapt from his cot. In front of him was this thing, sounding like his bunkmate flailing in the dark. He yelled, "Blinky, quit it, hold still," then pulled the tent off. He shined a flashlight onto the bleeding lip and wheezed, "What kinda ... Damn Blinky, he bit you right in the mouth!"

"Aiiieeeeee," they hollered and ran barefoot, in their underwear, crashing their way back to the main campsite. Their "Help! Help!" woke up the whole unit.

Blinky was crying, his eye twitching, his head jerking. He shouted, "He bit me on the lip! He bit me on the lip!" Whale turned in circles, mumbling, "What kind of deal is this? What kind of deal is this?"

The wild-eyed pair were so traumatized that neither the First Sergeant, the medics, nor the chaplain could calm them. They were loaded onto a medevac helicopter and flown to the post's hospital with Blinky's eye flashing SOS.

Whale Caldwell stayed in the National Guard for several more years. He got out just when his unit began training for civil disturbance duty. He never got above the rank of Spec Four.

Blinky Jervis got a medical discharge for bad nerves. He worked indoors at a cotton mill until the mill shut down years later. He was active in his church and had a reputation for helping folks out.

He passed away a few years back. Several members of his old Guard unit attended his funeral. One of them brought a box of salt.

They lagged behind after the others left and took turns pouring salt around the grave and snickering. They didn't see the big, red-headed man coming from behind them. Someone giggled, "Are we gonna pee now?" They hollered and then howled when The Great White Whale squeaked, "What kind of deal is this?"

CHAPTER 3

MARCHING BAND

One April in the early 1950s, the local school system in my hometown announced there would be a band program for the first time since the end of WWII. Companies that converted into plants making munitions had returned to manufacturing band instruments.

Salesmen came in slicker than the "Music Man". Open cases of trumpets, trombones, baritones, saxophones, clarinets, flutes, and drums were on display at the grammar school. The salesmen, whom the parents believed were experts, carefully examined the shape of each child's mouth to recommend the "proper" instrument little Johnnie or little Susie should play. It was part of their sales pitch, which included "easy payment plans" when cash was not available.

Over the following weeks, we smaller kids struggled to haul our instruments up the creaky stairs of our old middle school building for once-a-week rehearsals. We were in an auditorium with wooden seats and a small stage. The band director of a neighboring school came in to get us started. Despite a bad lung, which kept him out of the war, he was a really good trumpet player.

"Flip the seat in front of you and put your music stand on the floor in front of it," he said.

He pulled out his trumpet, did a quick warmup, and went through a short jazz rift. We were impressed. "Open your books to Lesson One," he told us. "Look at the Time signature." There was paper shuffling and "No, see right here, it's on page three" comments from students helping each other.

"See the time signature at the top of the page? The top number is the number of beats per measure, and the bottom one tells you which note gets one beat. In 4/4 time, a quarter note gets one beat, like this." He played four short notes on his trumpet. "A whole note is one note held for four beats." He played a whole note. "Now look at the rests; those markings tell you the number of beats not to play."

The first lesson was simple. We read the music score and screeched and blahhed a whole note, took a whole rest, then squawked four quarter notes followed by another whole rest.

Within a couple of weeks of whole notes and whole rests, the discipline of the group broke down. Older boys, bored with the drills, began blowing their horns at inappropriate moments. This guy did not mind.

In a short time, the entire group came to believe that it was OK to honk or tap out of turn, including the very moment the band director stepped onto the stage. We were unaware that music had protocols or rules. We kept honking until he waved his baton and told us to stop.

It was in this atmosphere that our newly formed band of grammar school and high school kids assembled to meet our new band director one steamy August morning. He was short and stocky with reddish curly hair, and of all things, he was a Yankee named Destazio who had come South from New Jersey.

When we arrived, someone had arranged folding chairs and music stands in rows, arching around a small riser. Attentive mothers sat in clusters around the gym as we took our seats.

Someone blew a trumpet; a clarinet player squeaked a sour note, and soon the entire group morphed into its undisciplined cacophony of blaring sounds and honks and drum tapping. The mothers thought we were so cute.

The new band director stepped onto the riser. Kids kept blowing their horns and duck-call squeaks. He stepped off the riser, and the noise grew louder. He stepped up again, and the kids made more noise. The third time, he flung a metal chair across the gym and yelled, "D!!@#$% it shut up." A couple of clarinet cases were snapped shut by little girls who ran crying to their mothers.

"From now on," he yelled, "whenever I step on this riser, you are to stop playing and look at me. Do you understand?"

A couple of kids sheepishly mumbled, "Yes, sir."

"Do you understand me?"

"Yes sir!"

This Yankee was fully in charge.

Over the coming weeks, we learned Pete Destazio was a WWII vet and had no qualms about using military techniques for discipline and enforcing musical rules.

He could do this because the band room was hidden behind the cafetorium and surrounded by a brick wall and hedges. It was the perfect location, away from the prying eyes of teachers and the principal. In this secluded building, he could apply what he believed were good practices to maintain order and build self-confidence.

Now, the school would not tolerate this, but none of us kids reported him because we knew he was not mean, he cared for us, and, besides, it was fun to go through it. He once caught a couple of boys giggling and punching while he was on the podium conducting. Quickly, he stepped down, walked to them, and asked, "You think this is funny? Assume the position to play." Then he snatched the chairs from under them with a "don't move" and left the boys squatting as he walked back to his podium and resumed rehearsing us and grinning. We loved it.

There were episodes of students standing on one foot in a metal folding chair, holding their instrument to the side for balance, and yelling, "I am an idiot; I played on a rest!" He caught a baritone player poking and punching his seatmate. "Get up here," Destazio ordered, "face the chalk board!" He looked at the student's nose and drew a circle a little higher. As the student struggled to stand on his toes, Destazio continued our rehearsal.

Those unable to accept his techniques ran home, complained to their parents, and dropped out. What remained was a cadre of band members who had a loyalty to him that bordered on idol worship.

Over the course of the August weeks, we spent mornings learning to march and play in formation. This was to prepare us for the halftime shows at the football games that fall.

Band uniforms arrived the first month of school. We had military-styled hats similar to those worn by Army Air Corps pilots during the war and white suede shoes with black rubber soles.

The uniforms were blue and grey, with Eisenhower-style jackets with white cording loosely worn off the left shoulder.

The night we made our football game debut, the band director said, "You have practiced hard; you look amazing. Just stay in line and watch the Drum Major. You will do well. Oh, one more thing: if you drop anything, do not pick it up. It will ruin the formation. Just keep marching and stay in line. We'll pick it up after you finish."

When the game paused for halftime, those of us in our new band, in new uniforms, formed a perfect square beneath the south gold posts. The fans rose, clapped, and hollered.

We stepped off in perfect formation. Just before midfield, the tenor sax player's music holder fell and scattered music onto the turf. The ten-year-old stopped—and bent over—in the middle of the band.

The musicians in the column stacked up behind him. What had been a perfect square suddenly had a tail.

"Damn it, Frankie, leave it!" one of them yelled as they ran to catch up. The crowd hooted. Meanwhile, the band director was stomping up and down on the sidelines, yelling the sax player's name and something about "going to kill you."

The head majorette led us into our planned routine. We marched single file into a spiral that turned inward, then back out into regular formation. When we finished, we marched to the sidelines to right flank off the field, one rank at a time. While each rank moved up, the bass drummer marched his bass drum right against the back of the errant saxophone player in front of him.

The saxophone boy's sash cord caught one of the drum's tuning knobs. As he tried to execute a right flank, the boy felt a tug. Rather than look back, he furiously jerked and twisted, then lost his balance and fell, pulling, with him, the bass drum and the bass drummer onto the ground.

It was hilarious. The head majorette helped them up and lifted the sash cord off the drum. The fans roared with laughter.

The sax player rushed to the school bus and sat on the steps, just sobbing. He was so embarrassed.

The band director walked up, put his arm around him, and said, "Don't cry, son; that was one of the funniest things I have ever seen."

CHAPTER 4

THE TWIST COMES TO TOWN

In the early 1940s or 1950s, some Southern Baptist preachers got the idea that dancing was immoral. These preachers were against it even though the book they worshiped from made no mention of it being against God's Will. Heck, the Old Testament said the Children of Israel danced, and Moses and David danced. So, what was wrong with it?

The Southern Baptist Convention never outlawed dancing, but it was devoted to the idea that Christians should separate themselves from the world's low-down ways. And low-down ways to these preachers included young people holding each other close and moving around when listening to music.

Now, this notion of avoiding temptation is not exclusive to Baptists. The Catholic Church, Methodists, Presbyterians, and other denominations also have their own lists of dos and don'ts. Episcopalians have a list too, but hand them a copy, and they would go, "What is this?" and set it aside.

Back then, Baptist preachers did not talk much about drinking and gambling. Drinking and gambling were self-evident evils with edges that cut and scarred lives and deep crags that destroyed many. But this dancing business was different. Dancing was soft, nebulous, and while in and of itself it may be harmless, in the wrong place it could become vulgar with titillating movements that could tempt the most devout.

Even though the Bible did not condemn dancing, it did tell the story of the king being so seduced by Salome's undulations that he got the head cut off of John Thu, the man for whom the Baptist Church was named.—That John-Thu thing might be wrong.—Anyway, conversations and sermons about dancing got so extreme, the joke was that people had stopped having sex standing up for fear someone might think they were dancing.

Heck, it was believed the spell dancing cast was so powerful it could lead pubescent boys and girls, mainly boys, to think about things they'd want to do with girls they'd like to do it with but knew they shouldn't.

So, it was in this repressive atmosphere of dos and don'ts that a local boy returned home from college. He showed up at the after-football-game party with a new dance ... the Twist.

To help him demonstrate, he found this attractive, more than amply apportioned, high school girl who, even better, had a reputation ... sort of.

The DJ spun a record, and Chubby Checker wailed, "Come on, babyeeeeeee!"

College Boy swung his arms and hips, twisting on the balls of his feet, leaning back, then ... in a manner never seen by the locals, he leaned, he actually leaned over his female partner, twisting, writhing, and butt shaking as if in some National Geographic mating rite.

Outraged chaperones sucked so much air out of the room, you couldn't strike a match in the place.

Baptist kids pressed their backs against the wall, grinning, then remembered they weren't supposed to enjoy this, then broke out in even bigger grins.

Methodist and Presbyterian kids were thinking, "How's he getting away with this, and how do you dance like that?"

Adult attempts at control fell apart as the dance floor filled with teenagers eager to master this new craze and loudly singing "Come on babyeeee..."

CHAPTER 5

CHRISTMAS ON SOUTH CHURCH STREET

For most of its length, Church Street in my hometown is wide and straight until it passes the water tower near the southern end. There it shifts left and narrows, squeezed between the embankment carrying the railway tracks on one side and the woods on the other. Past the woods, Church Street stops, blocked from crossing Marion Street by a small wood-framed house with big windows that, at night, glare back at intruding headlights. Just around the corner, South Church Street starts, then also stops, being boxed in by railroad tracks and trees. My family moved into the dead-end of South Church Street in the fall, about a year before I discovered the snare drum. I was nine.

The rhythm of the neighborhood was underscored by the movement of trains along railroad tracks, that most of the South Church Street houses backed right up against. Nondescript freighters and Seaboard Coastline passenger trains with names like the Silver Meteor, headed towards Miami, and the Silver Star, headed to Boston, and the east-west movement of trains from the Atlantic Coastline Railway marked the passage of time. The two lines crossed at a major junction, a couple hundred feet down from our house, and were governed by the blockhouse, a brown wooden structure of some height from which a switchman would operate levers and switches, sending the ACL trains across and Seaboard trains up and down.

The house my family moved into had a small yard that backed against a briar and brush-filled ditch right next to the Seaboard tracks. By late

December, my family and I had finally adjusted to the shaking doors, windows, pictures, and beds caused by passing rail cars to the point that these late-night rumblings had become cues to slide deeper into sleep. Even our dog had settled in, no longer circling, whining, or moaning at the sound of an approaching freighter. He still howled, though, when the train whistle blew.

It had been cold for nearly the whole month of December and dry. There had been no rain for weeks. Christmas morning dawned brightly with clear skies. The neighborhood kids poured into the street, playing with their Christmas treasures: punting a new football, riding a new bike, or pushing the new doll in her very own stroller. As the morning wore on, the new football showed noticeable scratches from hitting the pavement too often, and some toys had even been destroyed. One kid, struggling for some time to fuel, prime, and finally start the motor, had flown and simultaneously crashed his brand-new wire-guided model airplane in one giant, swinging arch.

At our house, I had followed my older brothers out the back door, attired as a cowboy, my new double holster cap guns buckled onto me, and wearing my Santa-gifted, official, Roy Rogers, white, good guy, cowboy hat. I knew it was an official copy of the one Roy wore in his movies because it had Roy's signature written onto the hat band in brown ink, resembling a cowboy lasso. Not another kid in the neighborhood had an official Roy Rogers white cowboy hat. I was set.

We crossed the ditch and climbed onto the railroad tracks to join some older boys who were tossing firecrackers. Being in their early teens, both my brothers, now safely away from our parents' eyes, had fired up cigarettes. At the time, lighting up was part of the social ritual for joining other boys who were smokers, and, besides, cigarettes were useful for igniting whole strings of Kats Paw miniature firecrackers set off machine-gun-like and punctuated by the occasional boom of a Cherry Bomb.

I forgot who, but as I recall, one of the older kids, with all the bravado a 14-year-old could bluster, said, "You boys ain't heard nothing," and pulled out an M-80, or as we called it, a TNT, the most powerful firecracker legally sold in South Carolina at the time. Taking a Pall Mall from his lips, he turned to the waiting group.

"This is what we used when we blew out the plumbing at the high school. This is powerful stuff."

Fingers went into ears. The lit TNT was tossed high into the air and fell hissing into the dried briars and leaves down in the ditch. *KER-BLOOMM-YOWW!!*—The explosion echoed to the veneer plant and back. "Damn!" and "Yeah!" the boys shouted and clapped!

The echoes could still be heard just as the brush pile in the ditch, a tender box after a month of no rain, burst into flames with a loud—*WHOOMP!!*—and quickly started burning toward the houses nearby.

My brother, the Boy Scout, snatched from my head my official white Roy Rogers cowboy hat. With great force, he beat at the flames until the underbrush had been subdued and flattened into a smoldering heap.

Straightening the hat and rolling the front of the brim the way Roy Rogers wore his, my brother, proud he'd saved the entire neighborhood, handed back to me my official "king of the cowboys" hat, pock-marked by twigs and beggar lice and smeared with black soot and grime.

"Don't worry, we'll put some dry cleaner solvent on it, and it will be as good as new."

My wailing could be heard for two blocks. Mothers came out back doors to see whose child was getting killed. Some men thought it was the fire department signaling volunteers.

CHAPTER 6

SNAKES

Springtime, way before Easter, we had projects due one Friday in Sarah Pegues' 8th grade science class. With obviously more important things to do, my best friend and I managed to postpone work on it until the week it was due. We figured there was plenty of time to get specimens, conduct research, and write footnoted papers to be turned in two whole days later.

We reasoned we could easily do it in one afternoon that included band practice for me, baseball practice for my friend, and viewing channel 8 in Florence to see what "Rocket Rick" was up to.

Now we, two smarty-pants boys, couldn't choose a simple project like making a volcano. No, not us! No way! A volcano was too simple for us. All you did was pack mud around a Dixie Cup filled with baking soda. Pour in vinegar, and a bubbling froth would spew, illustrating a chemical reaction and the fact that volcanoes erupt. Nor did we choose to fashion a wing of paper and balsa wood, showing how lift is created when air flows over a curved surface. No! Not us! Too easy!

My friend and I brilliantly chose to do our science project due in just two days on snakes. You know, asps, serpents—more craftier than any beast of the field—Eve's tempter, and damned to slither "on your belly." Additionally, we chose to do our science project, due on Friday, in early April, when the specimens we needed ain't really out and moving around in big numbers!

We fashioned snake catchers out of a forked stick and a staff to which we'd nailed a belt so we could loop it over a snake's head, capturing it with one yank. Thus armed, he and I set out for that field of clay that ran just beyond the houses in Wallace and back towards the river. It was a field where no decent snake would ever consider passing over or hibernating within. Wednesday was shot. We were sunk!

My friend's father came home from work that evening. After hearing our whining about how Sarah Pegues was going to kill us, he made a phone call to his boss. He told us his boss's son had a snake collection and would be happy to let us borrow it if we were careful with it. Yay! We were saved!

So, my friend and I showed up at school with a toilet paper case full of glass bottles. In them were a wide assortment of formaldehyde-preserved pit vipers, most of which were confined to the Okefenokee Swamp between South Georgia and Florida and not South Carolina.

For my paper, I did a pretty good rewrite of a section on snakes from the family's 1936 issue of Compton's Encyclopedia and the Boy Scout Handbook.

In getting the specimens, rewriting Compton's, and referencing, I focused all my time and attention on getting the science project done. I forgot my math homework. It was due the same day.

Sarah Pegues, who taught science and math, used every trick imaginable to translate obscure, dull concepts of mathematics into everyday applications, hoping it would inspire us to try to understand the subject she loved. She demonstrated how to calculate the number of square feet of a wall so a house painter would know how much paint to use. She got students to slide out a measuring tape to illustrate how carpenters used fractions when measuring the cut needed on boards.

She spent a lot of effort putting these subjects across and expected her students to do the same. When offended by their lack of effort, particularly with homework, she could scorch the earth, laying down a withering tirade that even made the older boys in class recoil.

The day our science projects were due, most of the class showed up without their homework. There was intense lobbying to have science first and math after lunch. This was to buy time to do it, or better yet, copy it off one of the smart kids. She bought it.

Students ahead of my friend and me showed their projects. Included was a Dixie Cup volcano that spewed foam off the desk onto the floor. The demonstrator was dispatched to the girls' restroom to retrieve paper towels to mop up the mess.

When it was our turn, we unloaded bottles of snakes. There were poisonous snakes floating in preservative and posing in aggressive, open-mouthed displays, revealing fangs and windpipes. Stacking them across Mrs. Pegues' desk, my friend and I, with angelic Tom Sawyer expressions, explained how the two of us had single-handedly captured, killed, and pickled each of the specimens displayed before them.

Emboldened by questions and skeptical comments from classmates, our avoiding bites and miraculous rescues blew up into life-and-death scenarios of epic proportions. Each snake was more aggressive and more dangerous than the previous one. Each capture was preceded by a near-fatal strike. We talked through five varieties of rattlesnakes, a cottonmouth, two copperheads, and a coral snake, which was rarely seen, if ever, in Chesterfield County. We managed to fill up all the time until the lunch bell rang. My friend and I were both pumped. We had pulled it off.

In the cafetorium, we were heroes. Other kids asked about our snakes. During lunch, we forgot we had not done our math homework. During lunch, we did not *do* our math homework. As the bell rang and we marched back up the stairs, Mrs. Pegues told my friend and me that Mr. Whitman had invited us to do our presentation before his science class right next door. Saved again!

Now secure in front of Mr. Whitman's class, we heard exclamations through the walls as Sarah Pegues discovered her students had not done their math homework. There was no way we were going back in there.

The stories we told earlier needed more content. We discovered the filibuster.

The details of finding and capturing each snake were expanded and stretched. We even added a twelve-minute sidebar explaining and showing the Boy Scout First Aid method for the care of someone bitten by a poisonous snake. Back then, the BS Handbook, Red Cross manuals, and other manuals said the best way to treat a snake bite was to cut an 'X' on each fang mark and suck the poison out.

Now, we're not sure when this changed, but the "suck the poison out" method may have been discontinued when some guy got bit.

As somebody told it, the guy was relieving himself when a copperhead struck. A friend was dispatched to a doctor for advice. The doctor told him to cut the 'X' marks and suck out the poison.

When he returned, the snake-bite victim was rolling on the ground and trembling. "What did the doctor say?"

"The doctor say you gonna die."

Thanks to questions from students, our presentation successfully filled the entire 40+ minutes needed to complete the last period of school for that last day in the school week.

So, it was April in either 1954 or '55. I think it was the same year I had to have an appendectomy, recited the Scout Oath on TV, and Junior hauled me on his motorbike to Dr. Thrailkill's office for stitches. I cut my hand trying to jump onto the roof of the bicycle rack behind Cheraw Grammar School.

PS: Sarah Pegues was one of the best teachers I ever had. She loved kids. She taught many of us how to swim. I can see her now standing on the pier at the state park, wearing that black one-piece bathing suit of hers, a white bathing cap on her head, and urging us to "kick your feet."

CHAPTER 7

THE PREACHER

At the beginning of my high school junior year, I got a job as a disc jockey at my hometown radio station. I was sixteen years old, smoked Marlboros, slicked my hair with Top Brass, splashed on Aqua Velva, and played drums. I was hot stuff.

Wary of me, my childhood sweetheart's mother shipped the love of my life up to a private girls' school in Danville, Virginia. She wanted to get her away from me in the hopes she might meet a better boy from a "Proper Family."

There were only two announcers at the radio station: *me* and the other guy. This was back in the late 50s, when Ike was president, cool cars had loud mufflers, and Jackie Wilson, Elvis, Sam Cook, and others were popular rock 'n' roll artists.

During the school week, I would wake up at five in the morning, sign the station on at 6:00, work until 8:00, then go to school and go back on the air from 3:30 p.m. until sunset. The station was a daytime station, and the FCC required us to turn the transmitter off at sunset.

The control room was in the same room as the transmitter, a 1KW AM device full of big tubes that glowed inside a cabinet almost the size of a large refrigerator. It had meters and dials on the outside.

The space in the control room was compact. You could sit behind the control board, reach across a turntable, and switch the transmitter on and off.

One hot August afternoon, I was on the air when a bad thunderstorm rolled in and—*KA-POW!!*—lightening hit the antenna outside. The bolt moved down the cables into the building and, in a scene similar to

Frankenstein's laboratory, blew out the transmitter with a loud blast, and flashes and sparks trailed away.

We were off the air for three days, which was good as it took me about that long to recover.

Back then, the radio station sold airtime to local businesses. There were times it sold to individuals—as long as they paid cash. Occasionally, the station would sell airtime to local preachers on Saturdays for cash—paid in advance. These preachers were not affiliated with the mainline churches. We carried the mainline services on Sunday mornings from the churches downtown.

The Saturday preachers were preachers who did not go to seminaries, study Greek and Latin, or, in solemn ceremonies, got robed in the vestments of ordained clergy.

These were men who suddenly got the call to preach from the Lord himself, usually after some cataclysmic personal event involving alcohol, bad checks, or the law.

So, for $14.95, they could buy fifteen minutes of air time, usually paid in small bills, nickels, dimes, and quarters. They figured that buying time on our station would help their small, independent "Bible-believing" churches grow.

I got accustomed to putting in 173 hours every two weeks, which included a split shift at the radio station and going to school in between. I got a day off every other Sunday. So, I figured I needed more activities on top of my cramped time between work and school.

What do you expect? I was sixteen and smoked Marlboros. My girlfriend, whom I really, really loved, was 150 miles away.

With nothing more to do, I traveled to Presbyterian Junior College in Maxton, NC, one Friday night to play drums at an event on campus. I got home really, really late. So, it was a struggle for me to get up at five that Saturday morning and go to work.

I barely made it through the morning shift. By the time the preacher showed up and paid his $14.95 for fifteen minutes of air time, I was really, really sleepy.

I took him into the studio next to the control room and asked if he wanted to stand or sit while delivering his sermon. "The Lord told me to stand when I deliver my message," he said, "that way I can really get into it."

So, I placed a lectern on the table and adjusted the boom microphone, then asked him if he was OK. He said, "Yes, praise Jee-sus," and I closed the door.

He was doing toe touches and knee bends to warm up as I returned to the control room. Looking at him through the plate glass window, I announced his name and, pointing to him, switched on his mic. He had fifteen minutes to sermonize.

I turned the control room speakers down several notches and said to my sixteen-year-old hotshot self, "I'll get a nap." I laid my head on the console, and the preacher began his fifteen minutes of air time with a moving sermon about "knowing the Lord."

Thirty minutes later, I came to. The preacher was into a crimson-faced, full-throated "Holy Ghost", shouting, screaming, and pleading. He beat on the studio window, then yelled at his radio audience and me, "Wake up, wake up, beloved! Wake up and repent of your sins!"

CHAPTER 8

KIMBERLY DAIRY

When my sixth-grade teacher was trying to teach us how to diagram sentences, she had me and one of the Lowery twins stay after school and write "I must not talk in class" one hundred times, nearly every day. We got caught and sentenced so often that we became adept at holding a pair of pencils on top of each other and writing "I must not talk"—two lines at a time.

School had just come back from Christmas break, and a classmate talked me into taking over his job delivering milk for the local dairy. This was back in the early 1950s, when milk came in glass bottles.

He said it was easy. The dairy truck would come by my house at five each morning to pick me up. We'd deliver milk, and then he would bring me home by seven-thirty, in time to eat breakfast and walk to school. On Saturdays, we made deliveries, cleaned the truck, did other things the dairy needed, and were done by noon. The dairy would pay us $12 a week, plus the driver would give us a penny for each empty soda bottle we found along the route.

Joining me was Red Burton, an enterprising fifth grader known for his pranks. He achieved fame when he slipped Ex-Lax to the bag boys at the Dixie Home Store one Saturday. As the rush hour of shoppers jammed the checkout lines on the store's busiest day, the Ex-Lax hit the boys full force. One at a time, they hollered, "Going to the back!" leaving the cashiers stuck bagging groceries.

It was cold that first morning when the dairy truck came to get me. Wearing a thick winter coat, I met the driver for the first time. He was an emaciated man who looked as though the Lucky Strikes he chain-smoked were shrinking him away from his clothes. He mumbled, "Mornin'."

He didn't say anything as he drove on down Church Street. If he had, I could not have understood anyway because he mumbled, and the ever-shortening Lucky never left his lips. We picked Red up, turned right on Christian Street to make it over to Market Street, and hung a left for our first stop that morning at George's Texaco gas station.

As we pulled up to the front door, the driver mumbled "Twelve half pints" and something else I could not make out.

Since it was my first stop on my first day on the job and I didn't want to appear that I did not know what to do, *and* I did not ask what his other instructions were. So, to make a good impression, I quickly gathered twelve half-pints of milk in glass bottles and hugged them against the front of my thick winter coat.

With great enthusiasm, I jumped off the truck, lost my balance, and stumbled into the front entrance. All twelve half pints, one bottle at a time, fell from my arms and shattered into an expanding pool of milk across the concrete floor.

Now, the driver spoke in plain English: "The basket, !$@%()##, I told you to use the #@%$!!!! basket!"

George roared. He said that was the funniest thing he had seen for a while and told us to go on, and said that he would clean up the mess.

I worked for Kimberly Dairy for several months with no more accidents. But on one cold, rainy Saturday in February, after jumping off and on the truck for several hours, I made a decision. I did not know what my life's calling was going to be, but I knew one thing for certain: whatever job I would take, it was going to be indoors.

CHAPTER 9

Did You Wet Your Pants?

A long time back—Lyndon Johnson could've been president—we had a family reunion at my uncle's house just north of Camden. My mother's family was large and gathered regularly to swap tales about kids and enjoy amazing food spread over several long tables.

Typically, there were at least three bowls of butter beans, three casseroles, rice, creamed corn, and a couple of trays of fried chicken, other vegetables, biscuits, rolls, and "Light Bread", as we called it. The chicken was homemade fried chicken, back before the days of KFC, Church's, or Bojangles. There were usually two congealed salads, several cakes and pies, and lots of iced tea.

My uncle's house was out in the country. The back yard was filled with kids: 4 to 5-year-olds, some 8-year-olds, and one self-conscious middle school girl who had that, "Eww, I don't want to be here; everyone's looking at me; don't look at me", look on her face. They were grandkids, cousins, nieces, and nephews, including my nieces and nephew from Columbia.

Card tables and chairs were set up in the back yard under a Chinaberry tree. I think if your background is working in retail, working with your hands, or if you are a Haigler or a Pate, there is a law that says you must have a Chinaberry tree. It must be because all my relatives had Chinaberry trees in their yards.

A short distance away were a barn and a small, fenced pasture where three horses grazed.

Sometime after lunch, one of the kids suggested that the horses get fetched so we could go riding. "Yay!" the kids shouted. My cousin, her husband Bill, and their small boy moseyed to the pasture to catch the horses.

We watched my cousin's husband dance back and forth in front of one of the horses, who obviously did not want to be caught. Finally, he got a lead line over her neck, and she stood still for him to get the bridle on her, but she did not like it. She was a red quarter horse that had not been ridden in nine months. That was nine months.

The horses were saddled, and my cousins and Bill mounted and rode them down from the barn at a walk and into the yard amongst the excited little kids. They trotted the horses out of the yard and down the highway a bit, turned, and at a walk came back to the house.

Bill looked down at me from this nervous filly and asked, "You want to ride?" To which my niece Anne, the five-year-old, said, "Yea, ride her Uncle Jerry, ride her Uncle Jerry!" I had no choice.

I climbed onto the saddle and gathered the reins. Bill says to me, "Now, she neck-reins," as if I knew what the heck he was talking about.

This horse was so uptight, she was quivering. The kids jumping and squealing didn't help; not to mention, the horse had not felt a rider on her in nine months. This mare was thinking, "I want to be away from this chaos. I got this dummy on me who doesn't know 'neck-rein.' I want to get back in the pasture."

We moved at a walk, out of the yard, and down the road for about a hundred yards. My cousins led the way, their horses gently clip-clopping along. My horse had her ears back, kept shaking her head and snorting. When we turned toward the house, she chomped on the bits and, with a mighty leap, tore down the road. She was low-running and looking for the barn.

I had a death grip on the saddle horn with one hand and was pulling on the reins with the other. I could not find a bass note anywhere, as I yelled, "Whoa and Helllpp!" We flew toward the house. My rear end was six inches off the saddle.

We passed the driveway, then she slid to a stop. I got her turned and rode her at a walk into the front yard. Her breathing was heavy, her nostrils were flaring, and she was making heavy noises. The kids came running up, and my niece Anne, the five-year-old, looked up at me and, with a gleaming grin, loudly asked …

"Did you wet your pants, Uncle Jerry?"

CHAPTER 10

THE FIELD FIRST SERGEANT

They had been standing in formation for a long time as the Company Commander, a First Lieutenant, had been inspecting every rifle, checking every gig line and belt buckle, and grilling every recruit on their General Orders. It was his final inspection before the unit graduated from basic training at Fort Jackson, SC.

The inspection seemed like it would never end. The company's snare drummer had been up way too late the night before consuming his canteen cup portion of Bourbon, which had suddenly appeared in the barracks. He was really short on sleep.

For eight weeks in the summer of 1962, he had done the double duty of going through basic training: running, push-ups, running, shooting, running, crawling, running, hand grenade throwing, running, bayonet jabbing, running, yelling, running, jumping, running, cleaning, running, and also playing the snare drum cadence that the basic training unit marched to.

Bravo Company, "Best of the Big Six" (B-6-2), was housed in World War II wooden barracks up on Ft. Jackson's famed Tank Hill.

Accompanying the commander on this final inspection was the unit's field first sergeant. He was a tall Master Sergeant whose training methods included using an oak limb to smack the bobbing helmet of an out-of-step recruit. As the platoon marched on, he made the errant soldier double-time around the platoon, holding his rifle above his head and yelling, "I am an idiot; I can't keep in step!"

On this last Saturday inspection, struggling from a lack of sleep and staring at the back of the head of the guy in front of him, the unit's snare drummer began nodding off. The company commander, with the field first sergeant looking on, was taking forever.

Finally, at last, the platoon sergeant yelled, "Third Platoon, huh-tenn-chunt!" The platoon snapped to attention. The commander marched up and turned. The drummer resumed staring at the guy in front of him and hypnotically began to doze again as the questioning resumed.

Just as the commander turned to face *him*, the startled drummer came out of his trance. He lifted his M1 rifle up to inspection arms and, for reasons unknown, turned it … upside down! He turned an M1 rifle upside down and was trying to hit the operating rod with his left thumb.

Here he was, a basic trainee, a private, and the company snare drummer, who had really, really screwed up!

Desperately, he turned the rifle over and slammed open the bolt. The Lieutenant snatched the weapon from his grasp and angrily peppered the recruit with dozens of questions as he checked the barrel, the receiver, the butt plate, and the muzzle.

With the recruit now really emphasizing "Sir! Yes sir!" as he answered and struggled to regain composure, the sergeant glared over the Lieutenant's shoulder and growled … "Pate, that's a sorry display of military form! You should have spent more time on the Manual of Arms and less time beating them #!!%%%!! Tom-Toms!"

Robert E. Jordan ran our company as the Field First Sergeant during basic training at Ft. Jackson back in the summer of 1962. It was a time when the Army scaled-down after Korea and before Vietnam became a household word.

Jordan was among WWII's Greatest Generation. He also fought in Korea and did two tours in Vietnam. He won a silver star and two bronze stars for heroism under fire. He was also awarded the combat infantry badge and a host of other medals before retiring at the rank of Command Sergeant Major.

CHAPTER 11

CHRISTMAS 1954

The week before Christmas 1954, the business district of my hometown was decorated with lights and candy canes. Music played over speakers mounted above the stores and offices on Market Street, including the outside wall of Dr. Funderburke's dental office.

As Bing Crosby sang "Silver Bells", Dr. Funderburke ground away at a bad tooth and interrogated me, with no real interest in my mumbled answers; he just wanted to keep my mind off his drilling.

Dr. Funderburke did not use Novocain for fillings; most of the time he reserved painkillers for extractions. Back then, dentists stood over their patients, used slow-speed electric drills, and had no dental assistants to hand them tools.

Patients actually took part in their own surgery by rinsing, then spitting water and dental shavings into a ceramic bowl around which a small stream of water carried the refuse away.

A master psychologist, Dr. Funderburke peppered his patients with questions. He got them to participate through commands like "turn your head over here and hold your mouth just like that." Then he would grind away, pause, squirt water in your mouth, and order "spit!"

By the time my filling had set—you had to wait for fillings to set— I'd heard the music cycle through Perry Como's "No Place Like Home for the Holidays" for the third time. When it was done, I rolled out the chair.

Accompanying me was my childhood friend Howard, who was startled, then terrorized, when Dr. Funderburke ordered, "Boy, get in the chair!" This was the early 1950s, a time when social norms required kids to say, "Yes sir, no sir, thank you sir." And for boys of eleven, you did what adults told you, and you didn't talk back.

Dr. Funderburke quickly gave "Mr. No-Cavities" an impromptu dental exam, after which we both flew down the creaky wooden steps and escaped out onto Market Street, where the magic of Cheraw, SC, at Christmastime calmed our trembling. Downtown was draped in garland. You could smell Christmas trees. The lights twinkled and danced to the music that played in the chilly air.

Howard, two other friends, and I had just joined the Boy Scouts that fall. Our troop, 653, had been selected to portray King Herod's soldiers looking for the baby Jesus during the Christmas Pageant at First Presbyterian Church.

My mother made me a costume from some old sheets, including carefully sewn pleats to give the skirt an authentic look. Our Scoutmaster, Douglas Watts, who had a talent for making things, found a novel way to fit us out with equipment.

Douglas was my hero. He and his twin brother, Gordon, were Marines during the war. Douglas would show up at Scout Meetings wearing a WWII aviator jacket with a fur collar and pencil slots and grill us on the Scout Oath and Scout Law.

To help our Troop have an authentic Herod's-soldiers look for the Christmas pageant, he made shields and shin guards out of cardboard spray-painted silver. They were strung together with twine.

For the Wednesday evening performance, we dressed and were issued our shields and shin guards. We looked as authentic a group of Herod's soldiers as Protestant southern white boys of British, Irish, and German extraction could look, despite our black and white, high-top PF Flyer footwear.

The lights in the church were dimmed, the music began, and in costume, Pete Destazio, our revered band director, began narrating … "And so, it was decreed by Caesar Augustus."

The choir began "Oh Little Town of Bethlehem" as a young couple playing Mary and Joseph carrying a baby entered the sanctuary from beside the choir loft. They walked over and settled into the stable on the other side.

The wise men came to talk with King Herod. He was sitting in the big chair where the pulpit stood. After they left, Herod summoned his soldiers. Our scout troop, now armed with cardboard-tipped spears, marched down the aisles, PF Flyers and all.

Having been ordered by Herod to search for this newborn King, we trooped out of the sanctuary and into the cold air, where our double-file, orderly marching ended. Now, with nothing to do, our troop morphed into a scrum of eleven-year-old boys jabbing spears and poking shields at each other.

After a couple of "Be quiets!" and a final "Gimme the spears!", the troop leaders collected our armaments and order was restored.

"Quietly" we were directed to re-enter the church, climb the stairs, and "quietly" sit in the balcony, where the poke, punch, and "quit it!", though somewhat limited, continued.

I remember the choir really sounded good that night, especially Helen Hamden singing the descant to Silent Night and Jo Anne Stubbs singing alto. I can't remember the cast for the 1954 pageant or much of the program, but I remember it being a memorable event in a town that becomes a magical place at Christmastime.

CHAPTER 12

MY BROTHER — MY HERO

There is a fabulous state park near my hometown. In the summer, teenage boys staffed the bathhouse and swimming area and looked after people, especially small kids. It was so safe that a mom could drop off her ten-year-old son and two of his pals at the swimming area at eleven in the morning and pick them up at two-thirty that afternoon with no problems. Besides the park, the town had high school athletics, Little League, Girl Scouts, Boy Scouts, and a myriad of other activities—except skating in an enclosed rink.

What skating there was, was done by little kids, scrunching along sidewalks on metal skates held in place by leather straps and toe clamps tightened by skate keys.

During the cold months, the town would occasionally hold skate nights in the main street business district. Here, folks could skate on asphalt. It was smoother than sidewalks, and skaters had no worries about cracks and bumps.

One summer, a portable skating rink came to town. It was set up beneath a circus tent on a vacant lot. It had wooden floors, and rink personnel rented shoe skates. They also sold skates.

After skating a couple of nights, my older brothers just had to have their own skates.

They bought them with the money they earned running GI Ray's hotdog stand. The stand was a tin shed made of roofing sheets. It sat between the Dixie Home Store and Melvin's liquor store.

On Saturdays at the back of GI Ray's, liquor connoisseurs took long pulls from bottles wrapped in paper bags, exclaiming ... "Hoooo weee, now that's smooth!"

Now, in my drinking days, I never found any straight whiskey I drank to be smooth. It burned like hell. Of course, I never drank for the smoothness or the taste. I drank for the effect, as my friends and those I annoyed can attest. —Anyway, back to my story.

My oldest brother bought some black high-top, leather-booted skates that he promptly spit-shined till they gleamed.

The rink drew big crowds of skaters, usually on Friday and Saturday nights. They glided around the floor to those awful, early, three-chord guitar, saxophone, and drum, rock 'n' roll songs played over tinny-sounding loud speakers. Nonskaters, mainly parents, stood outside next to the rails.

In a short time, my brothers were doing spins and skating with girls as if dancing. Other boys, who were good skaters, got to skate with girls that normally would not speak to them in school, much less hold their hands.

For some reason, most of the good skaters were real skinny. Not too many fat people skated. Come to think of it, there weren't too many fat people back then.

The skating rink also opened for matinees, where most of the smaller kids would come because it was safer and not too crowded. So, one afternoon, I showed up there with my two older brothers, who were going to show me how to skate on a wooden-floored rink. I was eight years old.

To them, I was their tag-along kid brother. They were my protectors, my superheroes, and at no time did I feel they didn't want me with them.

As they helped me lace up my skates, both of them were cautioning me to take it slow and be careful because ... "This isn't like skating on the sidewalk. This floor is slick!"

"I know, I know," I argued.

They helped me up and skated me over to the railings, where it would be safer for me to get used to the skates and the floor. "Grab onto those rails, take your time, and get your balance," they said, "and take it slow."

Well, I was up, and I was balanced. I made about three turns around the rink when—*BLAM!!*—I hit the floor.

As they skated over, "We told you to take it slow!" they yelled and started pulling me up. My left forearm was flopping.

"It's broken; you broke your arm!" they shouted just before they went into hero-rescuer mode. I had not made a sound—I must have been in shock.

They scooped me up, put me in a car, and all four of us sped up Front Street to the doctor's office.

Back in the X-ray room, I laid on a table. The doctor came back with the X-ray and said it's broken. All this time, my oldest brother, my protector, my comforter, was holding and patting my good hand. He was looking into my eyes, reassuring me that everything was going to be all right. I still had not made a sound.

The doctor turned on his fluoroscope, picked up my arm, and held it under the scope. He said, "This is going to hurt a bit," and—*SNAP!!*—he set my broken arm. I made a slight moan, and sweat broke out on my face. I never cried.

And my brother, the superhero, older brother, protector, and comforter—He stuck his head in a trash can and threw up.

CHAPTER 13

WEENIE BRAINED BOYS

It was early March; basketball season was winding down, and spring would be coming in a few months. Cold winds blew leaves into swirls, dried, blackened, and dead, and the day turned to darkness a little after six. As nature was heading towards another season, stirrings of manhood had begun to awaken in the boys at the high school.

For some, the change was gradual. For others, such stirrings were cataclysmic shifts, fault lines a mile wide transforming the football and basketball statistic-spouting teenage boys into the horniest bucks whose mental fantasies had them rutting through nearly every female they saw, teen-aged or adult, in the halls, in the classrooms, in the cafeteria, in the parking lot, and in the church choir. These guys were vaulting from young boys to young men. Their brains, induced by testosterone, were focused on IT.

Some older classmates took advantage of this by luring a couple of freshmen out to a remote spot on the pretense of arranging their de-virgining by way of a wild woman who had a jealous boyfriend. Among them was Turkhurst Thomas, the biggest boy and, since sixth grade, the school bully.

On the appointed night, the car carrying them wound through an area littered with toppled trees and dead limbs. Over them, dry, sharp-thorned vines grew into canopies that, in the dark, resembled mounds on either side of the rutted trail. Here and there, holly bushes were scattered about. The car pulled into a clearing at the rifle range back of the country club.

Just ahead was a car—her car—parked near a tall, sweet gum tree. The back door of the car slowly opened.

Turkhurst prepared himself and waddled forward with his pants around his ankles.

As he grabbed the door, a shotgun blast sent double-aught buckshot ripping through the top of the sweet gum tree and blowing spiny sweet gum balls onto Turkhurst's ass. Balls were also sprayed towards the boys standing several yards back. One of the conspirators fell over in the dirt, yelling, "I'm hit! My Goddddd, I'm hit! Help me, help me!"

"Aha! I got you now, you sons of bitches!" a voice atop the embankment yelled.

BOOM!!—Another blast of buckshot tore at the tree.

The boys flew in panic toward the highway, with one of them yelling, "Don't break my glasses! Don't break my glasses!"

Turkhurst, certain he had been shot, sprung from the car and bounced off the tree, desperately trying to run and pull his pants up at the same time. His condom got caught in his zipper and was waving like a pennant.

He caught up and ran past the fleeing boys. With one arm flailing, he plunged off the road into a mound of briars and was certain the enraged boyfriend of the woman was coming for him.

Turkhurst clawed through vines, limbs, and holly bushes, whimpering. He crashed forward, one arm blocking limbs and branches, the other holding up his pants. He flew across the highway into the brush next to the bridge. He jumped the creek and ran out of his shoe, that got stuck in the bank. Deeper into the woods he headed, avoiding the road, certain that the woman's crazed boyfriend was going to drive down at any moment and shoot him dead with a 12-gauge shotgun full of buckshot.

Now on one shoe, yelping each time his bare foot struck limbs and briars, he ran for his life. Turkhurst was in too much pain and scared to hear the laughter erupting back at the rifle range.

Two boys walked down from the embankment, whooping. One of them had a shotgun slung over his shoulder. At the woman's car, a tall boy stepped out, howling. Waving a bandanna over his head and, in a falsetto, singing "Hello boys" as he slapped the car's roof.

"Shit," a boy said.

"You sons of bitches! This ain't funny!"

"Did you see Turkhurst haul ass?" laughed the boy with the bandanna.

"We scared the shit outta you guys!"

"Shit!"

"Was that buckshot?" a boy stuttered.

"I told Freddy not to use buckshot, 'cause it was too dangerous … but noooo … he said buckshot made a bigger noise."

"It sounded like a cannon went off," said one of the boys struggling to breathe.

"It's a ten gauge. I had to use buckshot 'cause I didn't have bird shot. I aimed at the top of the tree. That was just plain luck. It splattered Sweet Gum pods all over you."

"You son of a bitch, I thought I was dead. Those things hurt. Damn it!"

"Aww, come on, fellas, it was a joke!"

"You screwed with us for three weeks about this! Shit!"

"Hell, if you boys hadn't been so horny and so stupid, we couldn't have done it. You believed everything we told you."

"What about the woman?"

"There was no woman. We got Jimmy to play the woman because we didn't think any of you would recognize his daddy's car."

"Freddy had the shotgun, and Toby, over there, was up on the embankment with Freddy to signal if someone else came up to the rifle range."

"How did you know when to shoot?"

"We could see all of you from the embankment," Freddy said. "We figured Turkhurst would go first. Toby wanted me to shoot when we saw him, but I waited till he grabbed the door. He looked funny as hell trying to run and pull his pants up."

"Where's Turkhurst?"

"He hauled ass!"

The group hollered and clapped.

"He was scared shitless when he came past me. I ain't never seen him like that."

"He was scared, real scared."

"We better go get him before he hurts himself."

There was a long pause.

Then, the smallest boy said, "Let him run! ... He's a bully!"

"Yea," said another, "he's a bully! ... Let him keep on running."

CHAPTER 14

THE MUMMY ON SHOCK THEATRE

In 1962, WCCA-TV in Columbia, SC, aired an 11:00 p.m. horror show on Fridays called Shock Theatre. It featured old Boris Karloff and Bela Lugosi movies and a cast of local characters who made live TV appearances during commercial breaks in the movies.

The director of this program was me, a Marlboro-smoking 19-year-old right out of high school.

The live studio segment of Shock Theatre had an ongoing plot featuring local talent portraying horror characters and was so popular that on Friday nights, people in Columbia would hold Shock Theatre parties during which the guests would turn the volume down during the Karloff/Lugosi movies, then turn it up when the live cast of characters would appear.

The host of Shock Theatre was a madman named Doctor Shroud, who conducted weird experiments, stole things, and terrorized the local community. His laboratory was inside the Happy Vale Sanitarium, a condemned asylum for the criminally insane. The facilities had been closed to the public for so long that the buildings were covered in Poison Ivy and Kudzu.

Dr. Shroud dressed in a dark cape with a hood. His macabre face and hands appeared to be decaying, thanks to the thick application of Hazel Bishop Number Five facial mask, which, when dried and scrunched, began to crack and flake.

A fawning, hump-backed creature called Igor helped Shroud do most of his dirty deeds. Igor had a horrible scar, so the story went, as a result of an eyeball transplant Dr. Shroud had performed.

Shock Theatre had no script. The dialogue, based on a story outline, was unrehearsed and adlibbed, from which a general theme ran from week to week that audiences could follow.

To set up camera shots, I took on-the-air cues from Dr. Shroud. Usually he said them in a Bela Lugosi voice, like … "Now we'll go into the operating room." This was the cue for me to tell one camera operator to "Follow Shroud" and the other to "Set up a wide shot in the laboratory."

Besides experiments, the plot of the TV show called for Shroud to employ an assortment of local characters to rob graves, steal cats, and create mayhem in Columbia neighborhoods and among students on local college campuses. Now this had the community theater crowd bombarding the station with story ideas and characters in the hopes they might appear on the program.

One of those was a woman who was a DJ at a local radio station. Short and attractive, she had long black hair and a bosom that could compete with Jayne Mansfield. For weeks, she called the station and lobbied to portray a lady vampire on the program. When Shroud took one look at her, he said, "OK." Then for two weeks, he mentioned a lady vampire would soon visit Happy Vale Sanitarium for the Criminally Insane.

The night she was to appear, there was only one camera operator to move two cameras. So, in preparing for the appearance of the lady vampire, I had the camera operator set up camera one on the host, Dr. Shroud, who would be on the air first.

Camera two, which was to pick up the lady vampire, was pointed in the opposite direction, with the camera operator standing between the two.

As the Bela Lugosi movie was reaching the place for us to switch and go live in the local studio, the lady vampire walked onto the set at the very last second wearing vampire teeth, red lipstick, a white negligee, and nothing underneath.

Just as we went live, the studio lights hit her, and the negligee became transparent. The camera operator says into my headset, "Damn! You can see clean through that thing." Dr. Shroud, who was now on camera, began giving me verbal instructions on the air with his normal—not Bela Lugosi—voice: "Eyes … focus the camera on the eyes of the vampire. The eyes of the vampire …"

We shot her from the neck up. You really could see clear through that thing.

This episode was topped several weeks later after Dr. Shroud announced he had come into possession of a mummy and was looking for a mad scientist to bring the mummy to life.

On the mummy night, a vicious thunderstorm hit the area. Heavy rain bounced off the tin roof of the TV station, and cracks of lightning and heavy booms of thunder could be heard in the studio—the perfect time on a live TV program to bring a mummy to life.

Somebody from the theater crowd found a real tall guy to portray the mummy—a guy who said he had never been on television, much less even been inside a TV station. He spent some time nervously giggling as the crew wound him in heavy gauze from head to toe. They left an opening around his right eye so he could see and move around.

As a Boris Karloff movie was running and the lightning was cracking, they led the nervous guy into the studio with him going, "What do I do? What do I do?" He was told to lie down on the table in Dr. Shroud's laboratory and to "Be quiet." His right side and right eye would be away from the camera.

The mad scientist, he was told, would stand just behind the table and face the camera.

Just before we went live, the nervously giggling mummy was told to be quiet and lie still until he was brought to life. No one explained to him how he was to be brought to life, and … no one asked him if he had any issues with hypodermic needles.

When the Boris Karloff segment ended, we cut to the studio with a camera and microphone on the mad scientist. The mummy was lying on the table in front of him. The mad scientist announced to the live TV audience, "It's time to bring the mummy to life." The mummy's right eye began to twitch.

The scientist held up this large vial we got from a veterinarian's office and jammed a long, heavy-gauge needle into it. It was attached to a large syringe—one of those big ones used for shots given to cattle.

Lightning cracked overhead, and thunder boomed. The mummy's eye was really twitching now.

As the mad scientist lifted the mummy's arm and pretended to inject him with the "Life-giving fluid," the mummy sat upright, shoved the mad scientist out of the way, and on live TV yelled, "Hell no! I didn't come here for this!"

He leapt from the table, screaming, and ran off the set.

I yelled at the camera operator, "Stay with him, stay with him," as the terrified mummy—on live TV—ran out of the studio, into the prop room, flung open the back door, and ran out into the lightning and rain, yelling in terror with gauze flapping in the breeze. It was beautiful.

It took thirty minutes to coax him back.

Regretfully, this was 1962, on a black-and-white live TV show with no way to record it.

CHAPTER 15

SMARTEST MEN IN "AMERICER"

Every morning across America, old men gather around tables at local restaurants or in the waiting area of barber shops to solve all of the world's problems. There must be some law that says geezers have all the answers to the world's needs.

Down in Greenwood, the owners of a restaurant hung a sign above the table where their local geniuses gather that read, "The Table of Knowledge." I asked a friend, "What qualifications must one have in order to sit at the table?" He said, "You need only one thing—an opinion."

I walked into a barber shop in Waco, Texas, one morning just as the local coffee klatch was in heated debate. These ole boys were not needing haircuts; they were there for the coffee and the sharing and consumption of great knowledge. One guy was so mad, he was red in the face. The two barbers were reared back in their big chairs, taking in every word.

When I walked in, the great debate stopped. The geezers looked at me, and I looked at them. Then I turned to the barber and asked, "Well, have they got it all figured out?"

"Oh, hell yeah," he said, "they just finished work on the North American Free Trade Agreement and have just begun discussions on whether bovine flatulence affects the photosynthesis of plants."

These pearls of wisdom are not confined to restaurants or barber shops. Country stores also provide informal settings for the locals to gather and impress each other with the depth and breadth of their knowledge, which expands each time a beer is drunk. I know this for a fact, as I have both seen and participated in great discussions ranging from the threat of North Korea to debates over which makes better bacon, a Duroc or a Poland-China hog.

When I lived out in the country—back in my smoking, drinking, and radio/TV days—I frequented such a place set right in the forks of two state highways. Early one afternoon, I pulled into the parking lot at Sarah Brown's store and noticed the local upholstery guy, whose truck was parked in the lot, had placed three signs advertising his business near the forks of the roads. Each sign, which was handwritten, misspelled the word "upholstery" a different way. That's three signs with the word "upholstery" misspelled three different ways.

No doubt this guy thought he needed to advertise since his biggest competitor, Nester Nixon, was on TV over in the city every night, puffing on a cigar and telling folks to "come on down to Nester Nixon's and save, save, save."

Now this local guy, the one who had put the misspelled signs out, was sitting inside Sarah's store when I walked in. Apparently, Sarah told him I was some famous radio/TV person, and because of that, this guy may have believed I was a friend of his big-mouthed competitor. This had to have been the case because, when Sarah introduced me, the guy acted suspiciously and refused to shake my hand. He squinted a hard look at me and asked, "Do you know Nester Nixon?"

I said no, but I had seen him on TV. The guy, still squinting, said, "Well, if you ever meet Nester Nixon, look upside his head. They's a imprint of a tack hammer ... I put it there."

Back then, the country was being roiled as social mores and customs were upended left and right. This was the 1970s, when Phyllis Schlafly was touring the country, warning America about a one-world government takeover if America ever gave women rights by adopting the Equal Rights Amendment, and Gloria Steinem was urging women to stand up and be heard. Folks were upset as customs about the roles of men and women were challenged at nearly every turn.

For the first time, men's barbershops had competition. New hair care businesses with exotic names like Mervin's Hair Process and places like Billy Bee's Beauty Parlor, which had become Billy Bee's Styling Salon, where both men and women are welcome. These new salons would shampoo, massage your scalp, cut, and style your hair, then fog it down with enough hairspray to keep it in place in a stiff wind. With all this change, it was only natural that traditional barbers became defensive about their craft.

A guy I worked with told me he had witnessed this firsthand. He said that when he walked into a local shop, the barber, who was clipping away, must have been upset that his college-aged granddaughter was going braless and his wife was complaining that their church wouldn't let her teach Sunday school above a certain grade. He said this had to have been the case because when he opened the door to the shop, the barber greeted him with this angry declaration: "Now, they's one thing we need to get straight before you come in here! This here is a barber shop. It ain't no stylin' salon. If you want your hair styled, get out! Go someplace else! If you want a haircut, it's 3 dollars. If that's what you want, take a seat and wait your turn."

Now, since I was a modern, macho, he-man American and knowledgeable radio/TV news reporter who favored the Civil Rights and Equal Rights Amendments, I had no problems when a friend suggested I try out a new styling salon. After all, other men I knew were getting their hair styled. So, I made an appointment at a ladies' beauty shop that had just switched from a beauty parlor specializing in beehive hairdos to a modern styling salon that served both men and women.

A nice lady washed my hair, massaged my scalp, and led me to a chair for my haircut. She informed me that she would not be cutting my hair but that their best stylist would attend to me. She seated me and put the robe around me, and as the stylist walked up, she said to me, "This is

Mr. Flambé, our award-winning stylist. Flambé, this is our newest customer."

As if he was watching a fashion show, Flambé steps back to check me out and, in a loud voice, greets me with, "Well ... helloo!"

The haircut he gave me was not a bad one. Although I never went back there, I did switch from my barber shop to a men's salon that offered a shampoo, cut, and style. This was before my hair fell out.

So, about three or four months after this "well hello" business, I was in Sarah Brown's store one evening after work, out in the country, reliving he-man stories and drinking beer with my friends—guys who were brick masons, carpenters, plumbers, and sheetrock hangers. You know, hardworking blue-collar guys who were smart and worked with their hands and backs.

I was seated with my back against the locked half of the door. I was listening, laughing, and taking part in our manly-men discussions. The door next to me swings open, and in steps the award-winning hair stylist—Mr. Flambé.

All talk stopped. It was so quiet, you could hear the motor running in the drink box. I'm praying, *oh god, please don't, please don't,* as Flambé eases up to the counter.

Sarah Brown says ... "Kin I hep ya?" The guys are elbowing each other and listening intently as Flambé says ... "I'd like a six-pack of Budweiser to go."

Sarah bags his beer; he pays, turns, takes one step, looks at me, and coos, "Well ... helloo!"

I wave hello, he leaves, and just as he gets outside, James Hutto says, "Well ... helloo!" The whole store erupts in laughter. I tried to say, "I can explain ...."

"I bet you can," they said.

CHAPTER 16

By the Road in His Underwear

Before political gerrymandering turned South Carolina into a state run more to satisfy party extremism than meet people's needs, four white men ran the state. Now, they took some personal liberties, but they actually got state business done.

Back then, a mayor got in trouble with his town council and was run off. Cronies at the Statehouse created a state job for him that was more about having a job than actually doing something. His main job must have been to keep a bar in his office beneath the steps of the Statehouse. Mid-morning one legislative session, a state agency representative opened the barman's door and quickly tried to close it. He saw the four white men drinking Bloody Marys. "Boy," one of them hollered, "I'm taking three million dollars out of your budget this coming year but will give it back the next." It was the Chairman of the Senate Finance Committee. That was it. No discussion, no bargaining.

A year later, the agency representative walked into the Senate Finance Committee just as its meeting started. The Finance Chairman saw him, turned to his assistant, and ordered, "Put five million more in that man's budget." That was the way things were done back then. These leaders looked after the state first, but then looked after themselves. They were all lawyers, and they saw to it that their law offices were on retainer by every major corporation in the state.

To celebrate his achievement that summer, the state agency Rep. rented one of those Silver Stream camper trailers. He towed it behind his car on a cross-country vacation to the Grand Canyon with his wife and two boys. They got a late start, and eight hours later it was dark as they were working their way through Tennessee. The Rep. was real tired when he pulled over and asked his wife to take over while he took a nap in the trailer.

She drove on for a couple of hours when her boys began fussing and poking each other. She jammed on the brakes and hollered, "Cut it out!"

When the car stopped, the Rep. jumped out the trailer in his underwear.

Unaware that he was outside, his wife drove off.

He later told friends, "You know, nobody will pick you up when you're trying to thumb a ride standing in your underwear."

After several cars flashed high-beam headlights and sped away, a long-haul trucker pulled over and said, "Get in, buddy; this has got to be good." They used a CB radio to contact the highway patrol.

An Arkansas trooper pulled over the wife and the camper and asked, "Ma'am, do you know where your husband is?"

"He's in the camper," she said.

"No, he's not. He's back in Tennessee—in his underwear."

CHAPTER 17

THANKSGIVING AT WIS-TV

Joe and I were working Thanksgiving morning, 1967/68, desperately looking for hard news stories we could do to fill Columbia, SC, WIS-TV's most watched newscast, The Seven O'clock Report.

We couldn't do national news as WIS-TV's prime newscast followed NBC's Huntley-Brinkley Report. And we refused to do soft news features like the origin of Thanksgiving, what Thanksgiving was like at Oliver's Gospel Mission, etc. when the police monitor reported an armed robbery at the Huddle House around the corner on Gervais Street.

At last, here was a real-news news story that we, real-news news people, could lead the Seven O'clock report with.

I loaded up a shoulder-mounted movie and sound camera with 16mm color film. The foul-smelling lab tech who processed our film, AKA the "green armpit," was sitting in the lobby watching the Thanksgiving Day Parade.

Joe, with microphone in hand, and I dashed around the building with the "green armpit" in pursuit. We were the first on the scene—the police hadn't arrived—and found the fry cook, an emaciated guy, standing outside, hands trembling, trying to light a Lucky Strike.

With the camera on my shoulder, I lined up a shot of the fry cook with the Huddle House in the background. I set the focus and told Joe, "We're rolling."

Just as he began, "Tell us what happened," a loud clacking noise came from the camera. The film had jumped a sprocket.

Before I could pull the camera down, the "green armpit" moved in and said, "I've got it." He opened the side door and, with his hairy pit up in my face, began to rethread the film. I thought I was going to die!

Joe looked at me, began laughing, then regained his composure, only to be struck by the appearance of this emaciated fry cook. The fry cook was trembling and sucking on a Lucky Strike as if his life depended on it. Joe's shoulders began to shake as he tried to keep from laughing out loud.

Joe had drilled me to never ask a "yes or no" question when doing interviews. The purpose is to get the subject to talk, and we needed this subject to talk because here on Thanksgiving Day there was a real-news news story. We really needed something to fill up the Seven O'clock Report, the biggest newscast of the biggest TV news station in South Carolina.

Joe giggled, "What happened?"

Fry cook: "We were held up!"

Joe tried again: "What happened?"

"We were held up!"

"Did he have a gun?"

"Yes!"

"What happened?"

"We were held up!"

"How much money did he get?"

"All of it!"

"What happened then?"

"He ran away!"

CHAPTER 18

SMART ALECKS AT CARDIO REHAB

After 20 years of jogging to stay fit and eating things with no taste, I end up in Providence Hospital for open-heart surgery—five bypasses. Once recovered, I was sent to the hospital's coronary rehab center, staffed by wonderful exercise therapists, a dietician, and nurses. There must have been close to twenty patients, mostly men, pedaling stationary bikes, walking on treadmills, and loudly talking over the machine noise.

The group was made up of a good cross-section of folks, including a divorcee who had been married to an Army Colonel. In short order, the patients bonded into a group, telling jokes and tall tales to fill the time as they trudged on treadmills or pedaled bikes. They also developed respectful, positive, and playful relationships with the rehab staff that grew closer to the degree that they felt they could play pranks on each other.

One afternoon, a patient swung by a drugstore on his way in and bought a camera and a pack of cigarettes. While a therapist was focused on helping a patient, this guy passed out cigarettes to several men and took pictures of them walking on treadmills, riding stationary bikes, and lifting weights with cigarettes stuck in their lips. The therapist went nuts. "What are you doing?" she grinned. "I've been trying to get people here to quit, then you pull … gimme the cigarettes!" The patients hooted.

The next day, the guy sneaks in and thumbtacks a poster made with pictures of the men exercising with cigarettes in their lips. Above them, he scrawled in big letters, "Providence New Incentive Program. The 5:30 group earns smoking privileges."

The next day, the therapist, who wore sneakers, shorts, and a T-shirt, elevated by an ample bosom, begins hollering and waving the poster at the patients. They were in the midst of telling jokes and tales. She hollers and waves, and the crowd does not react. Frustrated, she steps onto two chairs and yells, "What's it going to take to get you men's attention?"

A voice came back, "Take your shirt off."

She yells, "Look at this," holding up the poster and trying not to laugh. "Somebody put this on our bulletin board." Then, getting serious, she said, "Yesterday this was up there when the accreditation inspectors were here. We had to explain to them that you guys did this. This was not funny."

On Mondays during the football season, late-arriving men would walk in, warm up, get on a bike, and ask, "What quarter is it?" as the others relived games. The loudest among them was a bearded fellow of good size who was a Clemson fan. Here he was in cardiac rehab in Columbia, SC, home of the University of South Carolina, and he was a Clemson fan.

Robert could recall almost every play Clemson made and nearly every play by the USC Fighting Gamecocks. He sold big heavy equipment tires, was also a builder, and knew a lot of stuff. He was not a bit shy and had as many opinions as a conservative talk show host. A friend once described him as one of those guys who, "If he thought it—it came out of his mouth."

A couple of times each week, his attractive wife would join the group, usually to walk on a treadmill next to him. She was petite, demure, quiet, and overshadowed by her husband's larger-than-life personality.

Weeks rolled by with more walking, pedaling, rowing, and lifting, and a couple of episodes of diabetics getting groggy with low blood sugar, which the nurses quickly fixed with crackers and orange juice. The group bonded. We looked forward to seeing each other and listening to or telling tall tales, particularly about growing up in Columbia. Somebody began talking about going to the El Roco Club, the Owl's Club, or Doug Broome's drive-in restaurant with the carhop girls dragging their boots because Doug bought only one size, very large, to fit any girl who wanted to work.

During this discussion, somebody introduced the topic of the day: "Where were you the first time you did IT? Not it, but IT." 'IT' resulted in a rundown of various places, with each recount concluding with laughter. It worked its way through all the men until we got to Shirley, the Colonel's ex-wife. With gleeful anticipation, she took first place when she giggled, "In the back seat of a Packard at the Twilight Drive-In."

Notably silent was Robert, the "If he thinks it, he says it" guy. His wife was pedaling a stationary bike and watching to see what he would say.

"I ain't gonna talk about my first time," he said, "but I'll tell y'all Denise saved my life."

"What?" somebody asked.

Denise responded, "I took him off the street." To which enquiring minds wanted to know more details.

"He was a bouncer at a couple of clubs, and some women were throwing themselves at him. He started dating me, and that all stopped."

"Hell, if she hadn't done it," Robert said, "it's no wonder what kind of infection I'd be walking around with."

A few weeks later, we began discussing law enforcement. Robert told the group, "Hell, I knew nearly every cop around. Red Lanier gave Denise away when we got married."

He explained they had this big wedding at a big church packed with family and friends and nearly every cop, deputy, or trooper in the area, including the head of the highway patrol. Denise's sisters were bridesmaids, and Robert's groomsmen were his brothers and friends from law enforcement.

The wedding reception was held at the Ladies Club downtown, right next to the University of South Carolina campus. There was a big cake and lots of champagne and dancing and jokes, including Robert telling his buddies they better not try to put him in jail as a prank.

When the wedding reception thinned out, the bride and groom got into Robert's jeep and headed for Crockmeyer's Saloon on the other side of town—still dressed in their wedding attire. The rest of the bridal party was in pursuit—also formally attired.

As Robert sped through the university campus, he made a quick right-on-red turn, and a university cop flipped on his lights to pull him over. Thinking he had been pranked, Robert kept going and did not stop until the cop began wailing the siren, pulled beside him, and motioned for him to pull over.

"You going to take me to jail?" Robert chuckled, thinking he'd been set up by a friend who was a university cop.

"Not yet," the cop replied, then said, "I'm gonna give you a breathalyzer test first."

"For what?"

"You smell like you been drinking."

"I had three glasses of champagne at the wedding reception, and my buddies sprayed me in the face with it, and it got on my Tux. I'm not drunk."

"If the breathalyzer says you aren't, then I'll let you go."

"Alright, this has gone far enough. Did Pedro put you up to stopping me?"

"No, I stopped you for failing to stop when I put my lights on."

"You're serious?"

"Yep, now get out the jeep and stand next to it so I can test you."

"I ain't drunk, and I ain't taking no breathalyzer test."

"Then get out the jeep, turn around; you're going to jail."

Despite Robert name-dropping every cop he knew, including the head of the highway patrol—"who gave my bride away"—he was handcuffed and loaded into the back seat of the university cop's car.

There was more arguing of "What about my wife? She can't drive a stick shift," until a friend of Robert's came out of a drugstore and walked over. The friend offered to drive the bride while the cop hauled Robert away.

So, the bride, still wearing her bridal gown and a crown of baby's breath flowers on her head, shows up at police headquarters. By now, the groomsmen, still formally dressed, had joined her.

The desk sergeant was taken aback when the wedding party, including the bride carrying her bridle train over her arm, shows up.

"Can I help you, ma'am?"

"I came to get my husband out of jail."

CHAPTER 19

THE BAND BOYS GO RABBIT HUNTING

It was fall, before the first big cold snap. Cotton fields had been picked clean, and tobacco had long been harvested, cured, and sold. It was back when the Warren Court had ordered an end to school segregation, Senator Joe McCarthy was forced to stop his witch-hunt for communists, and the football season for the hometown team was mercifully coming to an end.

The team was made up of 20 boys, some of whom weighed 112 pounds in a sport that required muscle and bulk, and 11 players on a squad. They had just enough players for one team and nine substitutes. They lost more games than they won.

Most of the big guys on the team had to play whole games on both offense and defense, as the substitutes available were much, much younger and not much bigger than the 112-pound guy. And besides, there were only nine of them sitting on the bench. The team found itself mainly playing defense that year, as the offense didn't keep the ball long enough to score often.

For the most part, though losing close games, the team held its own as most of the other opponents in the hybrid conference of small schools and large schools also had limited squads, and their boys played entire games on both offense and defense. The conference wasn't aligned fairly, but it was the mid-1950s, and that's the way things were done back then.

The hometown team got smeared by those bigger schools with enough players to have an offensive unit and a defensive unit. The second half was usually a rout, as the home team linemen's legs got weary.

Marching band season was also ending. The band that year had managed halftime performances without any major hiccups, except for that time a young clarinet player forgot to do a to-the-rear march and found himself alone in the middle of the field as the band moved on. He had to run madly to catch up. The crowd applauded, and someone yelled, "Look at him go! Put that kid on the football team!"

Then there was that night, when the big halftime show had the band forming a circle, and the lights were shut off on the football field so the head majorette could twirl a fire baton.

The band didn't play because they couldn't see their music. Actually, when bands didn't have much of a halftime show, they'd hoodwink the crowd with a fire baton display. So that night, the lights were off, the fire baton was lit, and the drummers flipped their snares off and beat their drums as tom-toms on the four beats. The first beat accented rhythm the way white guys in wigs played Native American Indians in John Wayne movies. The crowd went wild.

That night, the football team was down by two touchdowns at halftime, and the crowd was anticipating the big smear in the second half. The halftime show ended—but halftime didn't.

They couldn't get the lights back on. No matter how hard they tried, they couldn't get the ballpark lights on. Thirty minutes later, a power company lineman showed up and climbed the pole, got the connection for the lights fixed, and the game resumed. At that point, our team had nearly an hour-long break, including a nap, and returned to the field rested and eager to settle the score. They won by one touchdown.

Now the band had a couple of members who were football-sized boys but who preferred playing instruments to football. This really frustrated the football coaches.

The band didn't require you to knock someone over or run wind sprints. Plus, in the band, you could be around girls, good-looking leggy majorettes, and girl clarinet players. And you got to ride with them on the band bus to and from games, especially the out-of-town games.

The head coach spent four years, with no success, trying to recruit the band's bass horn player to play football. The bass horn player was a big guy. He was tall and had such a muscular physique that he could have modeled for the Charles Atlas body-building course. He was one of the best musicians in the band and had no interest in giving that up to play football.

Football season was over, and four of us band-member boys decided we'd go rabbit hunting after band practice—with shotguns.

The bass horn player, who was the oldest in the bunch, got a farmer to let us walk his property in search of "Thumper" or any of his kin we could scare up. We didn't have beagles to help us. We just plowed through briars, dead tree limbs, and other underbrush, carrying our shotguns and talking loudly, driving any animals, reptiles, or birds to safety well ahead of us.

We walked and talked almost until sunset with no success and decided to pile into the car for a final attempt at spotting a rabbit alongside the road. The car was a Packard, one of those long, low ones with a heavy front grill and a shape like a Hudson Hornet. I think it was one of the last ones Packard manufactured before going out of business.

The game plan called for two guys with shotguns to straddle the headlights on the car's hood with their feet on the front bumper for balance. We hoped the headlights would pick up and freeze a rabbit in place long enough for someone to get off a shot.

Now this process ain't fair to rabbits, and it ain't legal either, but we were teenagers, had raging testosterone—and were bullet-proof.

The four of us took turns driving and straddling the headlights.

Finally, two guys spotted a rabbit and fired shots, with both of them missing. One of the boys jumped off the moving car, believing he could catch up with the rabbit easier on foot than riding on a car. He fired two more shots, missing both times. At this point, the driver, the bass horn player, stopped the car and told the boys to get in because it was time to go home. They handed their guns through the windows into the back seat and got in the car.

As we drove along the country road, my seatmate observed, "You know, I haven't fired a shot all day." Then, with no warning, he poked his shotgun out the rear passenger window with the barrel alongside the driver's head and—*KER-BLOOM-YOW!!*—fired the gun. We almost wrecked. There were no injuries.

—We were bullet-proof, in the band, and got to ride with the girls on the band bus.

CHAPTER 20

"Hippatized by Perfesser Zeeto"

Back in the 1950s, before big-box stores killed small businesses, merchants of family-owned businesses and regional chain stores made a living in the downtown area of Market Street and Second Street in my hometown. There was a time when Market Street, from Front Street to Second Street, had four grocery stores, four clothing stores, three drug stores, a Five & Dime, a bank, and a savings and loan all squeezed into that one block that also included a dentist's office, a doctor's office, a cotton brokerage, G. I. Ray's hotdog stand, and a liquor store.—I may have missed some businesses, so don't write letters to the editor complaining I left something out because this ain't a news report, it's a tale.

Back then, when Ike was President, merchants promoted their businesses by buying ads in the Chronicle or radio spots on WCRE, which had just gone on the air. Mainly, though, most merchants put displays in their windows and big posters announcing sales on slop-jars, women's girdles, men's work shoes, or plow lines for mules.

There was one men's clothing store downtown, Hamilton's Men's Wear. The owner carried a special line of men's apparel not readily available in the department stores and did a good business because he had a unique way of promoting it. One of his salesmen was the town magician, radio disc jockey, and hypnotist all rolled into one. He went by the stage name of Professor Zeeto.

Professor Zeeto gained fame one night on the stage of the old high school auditorium when he single-handedly escaped from an official

United States Postal Service mail bag after being locked in it by the Postmaster himself. Professor Zeeto was a sensation.

He was also a promoter. He convinced his boss that he could draw a crowd of customers to the men's clothing store by hypnotizing some guy and laying him to sleep in the front window wearing an outfit from the store with sale signs stuck on the inside wall. They would get the local funeral home to lend them one of the gurneys they used when hauling corpses, and they would use that for the participant to lie on. The gurney was a perfect fit for the front window.

They spent a week, with no success, trying to talk men into participating in this historic event. As a last resort, they turned to schoolboys and found a sixth-grader willing to be put under Professor Zeeto's spell. Sixth-grade boys will do anything.

On a Saturday afternoon during the winter, when it gets darker earlier, the sixth grader shows up with three of his giggling buddies. They dressed the boy in a new shirt, pants, belt, socks, and shoes.

Professor Zeeto had the boy sit on the edge of the gurney, and after telling his giggling pals to be quiet, he got his subject to stare at the pocket watch, which he began swinging back and forth in front of the boy's face. "Pay attention to the watch and listen only to my voice," Zeeto quietly intoned. "Your arms and legs are getting heavy. Your eyelids are getting heavy. You want to go to sleep." The boy stared at the watch, began to relax, and, after a few short minutes, was asleep. "You are completely relaxed now. Listen only to my voice," Zeeto instructed. "Lie back and relax."

With the boy stretched out, the gurney was lifted and placed in the front window feet first, so the onlookers would have to walk in towards the store to see the boy's face. It wasn't long before a crowd formed, and comments were made. "Dang, look at that boy. Is he dead?"

"No, he ain't dead," one guy said. "He's been hippatized."

Now in every group, there's that one person who knows everything, has seen everything, and has done everything. All he needs is an audience, and he becomes an expert.

"He ain't dead; he's hippatized," the guy said. "That Perfesser Zeeto in there—he's the one that done it. That boy will do anything Perfesser Zeeto tells him. I know what I'm talking about. Once you get hippatized, you're under the complete control of the one who done it, and they ain't nothing you can do about it.

"I seen a magician at a Hoochie Coochie Show at a carnival once who got a woman to come up out of the audience. He hippatized her and told her to take her clothes off in front of everybody and dance up on the stage. I seen him do it. She was dancin' and dancin', and when the music stopped, the magician snapped his finger, and she come to.

"She hollered and slapped that magician a good one and told him to give her her clothes back. She wasn't all the way nekked, but she was shore upset. You ain't got no control when one of them magicians puts you under a spell like that boy in the window. I know what I'm talkin' 'bout."

ABOUT JERRY DEAN PATE

Jerry DEAN Pate is a retired trade association president and executive. He spent some thirty years lobbying Congress and state legislatures on behalf of the telecommunications industry and electric cooperatives. He holds a Bachelor of Arts in Journalism degree and a Master of Public Administration degree from the University of South Carolina.

A South Carolina native, he also worked twenty years in radio and television as a reporter, writer, producer, news anchor, and news director, covering the state legislature, the Civil Rights Movement, and women's movements from the mid-1960s onward.